THINGS TO DO

THINGS TO DO

By Elaine Magliaro   Illustrated by Catia Chien

chronicle books · san francisco

Things to do if you are DAWN

Shoo away night.

Wash the eastern sky with light.

Wake the sleeping sun:

Rise and shine!

Rouse resting roosters.

Set songbirds singing.

Let dreams *drift away*.

Start a new day.

Things to do if you are 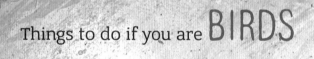 BIRDS

Go find your breakfast.

It's strewn on the lawn.

Better come get it

before it's *all gone!*

S t r e t c h out your wings

on the brightening sky.

Morning's upon us.

Get ready to *fly!*

Things to do if you are a HONEYBEE

Flit among flowers.

Sip nectar for hours.

Be yellow and *fuzzy*.

Stay busy.

Be *buzzy*.

Things to do if you are an

ACORN

Wear a bumpy, round cap
and a starched brown coat.

Grow plump, ripen,

snap from your stem . . .

. . . AND OFF YOU GO!

Fall to the forest floor below.

Tempt a scavenging squirrel.

Let him bury you in a bed of earth

    beneath a blanket of moldering leaves.

Dream the winter away.

Then, in spring,

        sprout.

    Let a little *oak* out!

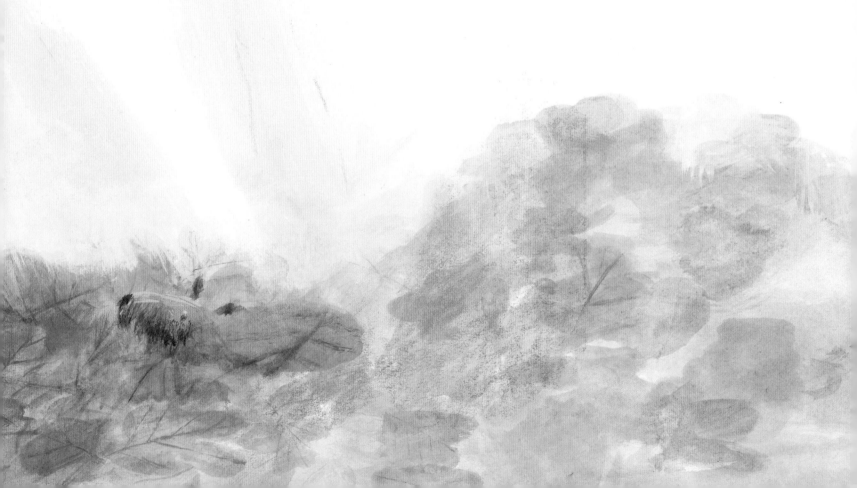

Things to do if you are a SNAIL

s l o w l y . . . *s l o w l y . . .*

take your time.

S l i d e along your trail of slime.

The wonders of your world are small.

Don't hurry by.

Enjoy them all.

Things to do if you are the SUN

Be *big* and round

and *bold* and bright.

Wear a crown

of golden light.

Shower down

warm yellow rays.

Rule the sky

on summer days.

Things to do if you are the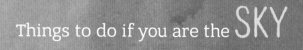

Stay clear and blue.

Let the sun *smile* down.

Don't grow grumpy,

gray, and frown.

Don't *scramble* storm clouds.

Don't grumble and complain.

Don't *stab* the ground with lightning.

Don't rain!

Don't rain!

Things to do if you are an

ERASER

Be pliable and pink.

If I draw *before* I think,

rub out *every* mistake

that I happen to make.

That's what your job's all about.

Go on—

wear yourself out!

Things to do if you are SCISSORS

Open wide your silver jaws.

Then snap them shut.

Open.

Shut.

Open.

Shut.

Snip, snap, snip.

Action: *Cut!*

Things to do if you are

Polka dot sidewalks.

Freckle windowpanes.

Whoosh down gutter spouts.

Gurgle into drains.

Patter 'round the porch

in slippers of gray.

Tap dance on the roof.

Then . . .

go away.

Things to do if you are BOOTS

Splish in puddles.

Splash on the walk.

Make the fallen

raindrops *talk*.

Things to do if you are an
ORB-SPIDER

Weave a web of silken strands

with spinnerets

(*you* don't need hands)—

a silver net . . . a sticky snare . . .

a clever trap that's light as air.

Weave a web . . .

then watch and *wait*

upon your woven dinner plate.

No need to *hunt* to catch your prey.

A meal will soon be on its way.

Things to do if you are CRICKETS

Quiet

fills this summer night.

Fireflies

dot the dark with light.

Birds

are nestled in the trees.

The world is still.

There is no breeze.

Tune

your instruments and sigh.

Bid

this balmy day good-bye.

Rub wings

and sing

a lullaby.

Things to do if you are the MOON

Live in the sky.

Be *bold* . . .

OR

be shy.

Wax and *wane*

in your starry terrain.

Be a circle of light,

just a sliver of white,

or *hide* in the shadows

and vanish from sight.

Look like a pearl

when you're brim-full

and *bright.*

Hang in the darkness.

Dazzle the night.

For three special ladies who bring joy into my life—my daughter,
Sara, and her daughters, Julia Anna and Allison Mary

And with special thanks to Grace Lin —E. M.

To my favorite person and my love, Mike —C. C.

Text copyright © 2016 by Elaine Magliaro.
Illustrations copyright © 2016 by Catia Chien.

Library of Congress Cataloging-in-Publication Data

Magliaro, Elaine, author.
 Things to do / by Elaine Magliaro.
    pages cm
 Summary: Told in rhyming text, the story takes us through a child's day,
focusing on the animals and objects around the child.
 ISBN 978-1-4521-1124-7
 1. Stories in rhyme. [1. Stories in rhyme.] I. Chien, Catia, illustrator. II. Title.

PZ7.1.M34Th 2016
[E]—dc23

2014028019

Manufactured in China.

MIX
Paper from
responsible sources
FSC™ C008047
FSC
www.fsc.org

Design by Jennifer Tolo Pierce.
Typeset in Bandera Pro and Denim.
The illustrations in this book were rendered in acrylic.

10 9 8 7 6 5 4 3 2 1

Chronicle Books LLC
680 Second Street
San Francisco, California 94107

Chronicle Books—we see things differently. Become part of our
community at www.chroniclekids.com.